WALT DISNEP PICTURES

PRESENTS

THE LITTLE MERMAID

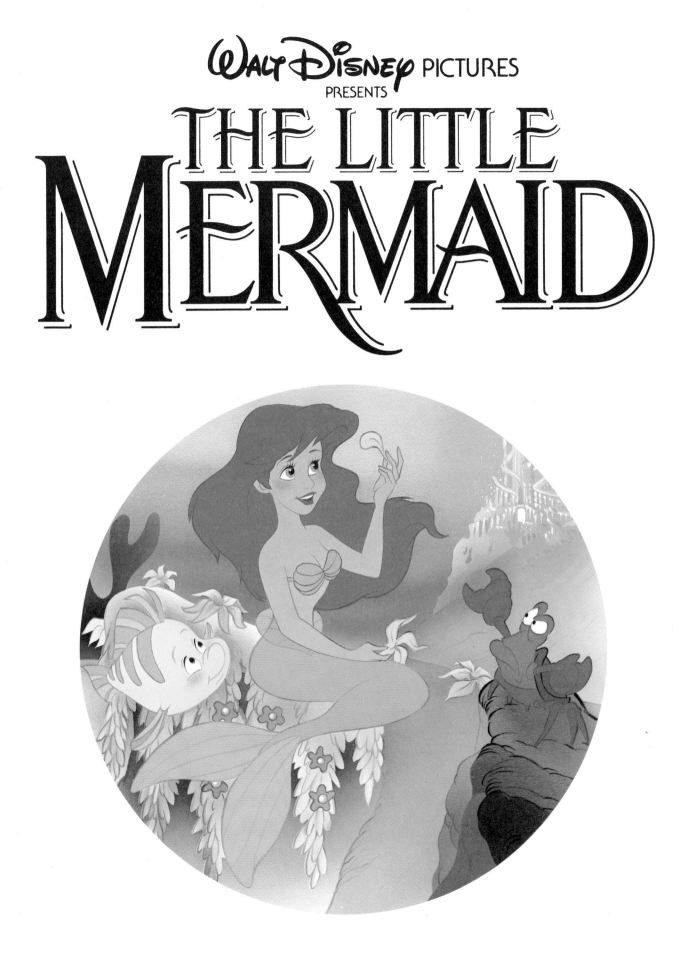

Twin Books

Ariel was sixteen, the age when a mermaid was supposed to be thinking about marrying a merboy and settling down. But Ariel had other things on her mind.

However, let's start at the beginning…

It was the day that all King Triton's undersea kingdom had been waiting for. Princess Ariel, the Little Mermaid, was going to sing. Ariel had the most beautiful voice in her father's kingdom. When she sang, everyone came to Triton's shimmering castle to listen.

They came from all over the ocean. Flying fish flew in. Swordfish made it a point to be on time.

And soon, they were packed into the Great Hall like sardines (which, of course, some of them were). Simply everyone was there.

Everyone except Ariel.

"Where is Ariel?" King Triton roared.

Ariel's six mermaid sisters shrugged their tails and said they didn't know.

"My concert is ruined!" wailed Sebastian the crab, holding his head in his claws. He was the castle's Music Director.

Everyone in the Great Hall looked at each other and said, "Where's Ariel?"

Far from the commotion at the castle, Ariel was doing her favorite thing—exploring the ruins of a sunken ship…a ship that had once belonged to the strange and wonderful world of humans.

Ariel picked up two objects from the ship's deck.

"What do you suppose humans do with these?" she said to her best friend Flounder.

"We r-really shouldn't be doing this, Ariel," Flounder replied nervously. "W-we're looking for trouble."

Neither Ariel nor Flounder noticed that trouble was looking for them, too.

Trouble came with razor-sharp teeth.

"Oh, no! A sh-shark!" Flounder squealed, darting here and there, away from the menacing jaws!

"Quick, Flounder! Follow me!" Ariel called, swimming with all her might toward a large anchor ring.

The Little Mermaid and the frightened Flounder slipped
easily through the ring. The shark plunged after them.
Oof!
Halfway through the ring, the shark discovered he was bigger
than the ring. The iron band held him like a giant handcuff.

The next stop for Ariel and Flounder was Scuttle's rock.

"Look what I found, Scuttle," Ariel said, showing the seagull the strange objects from the sunken ship.

"Human stuff, huh?" Scuttle said. "Lemme see. I'm an expert on human stuff."

"Humans call this a dinglehopper," the expert proclaimed. "Humans use it for...um...combing their hair."

Actually, the object was a fork. But only a human could have told them that.

Flounder was getting nervous. "Ariel, something tells me we should have been home by now."

"Oh my gosh! The concert! I forgot all about it. Father will be furious!" Ariel plunged off Scuttle's rock and swam as fast as she could for the castle.

Meanwhile, in a deeper and darker part of the ocean, Ariel was being watched. Jealous eyes followed the Little Mermaid. Now banished from Triton's palace, Ursula the Sea Witch plotted her revenge.

Ariel had never seen her father so angry.

"The whole kingdom is waiting to hear you sing," he stormed, "and where are you? Poking around shipwrecks, looking for human junk!"

"But Father…" Ariel started.

"Silence! You are never to have anything to do with humans again. Never!"

16

After Ariel had left the King's chamber, Triton thought for a moment. "I wonder if I was too hard on her," he said. "Maybe she just needs someone to keep an eye on her."

"I'll see if I can find somebody," Sebastian said helpfully.

"I've already found him," Triton said, pointing at Sebastian. "You."

"Why me?" Sebastian muttered. "I'm a musician, not a nursemaid. Now, where did that girl swim to?"

Suddenly, he heard Ariel's voice coming from a half-hidden cave. He scuttled over and peeked in. There she was, talking to Flounder. All around her were human treasures.

"Oh, Flounder—if only I could be part of the human world!" she sighed.

Sebastian gasped. He was just about to step out of his hiding place and speak to Ariel when, without warning, the cave went dark. Something on the surface of the water was blocking out the moonlight.

"A ship," Ariel cried, swimming straight up.

"No, Ariel!" Sebastian shouted. "Come back! Your father..."

But Ariel was gone.

Many times before, Ariel had seen ships. But she had never been able to swim close enough to see the humans who sailed them. Now, her eyes wide, she saw them!

Some were laughing. Some were dancing hornpipes. Some were making music. And some were saying, "Happy birthday, Prince Eric," to a very handsome young man.

"Thank you all for the statue," the young man said. "It's really something."

The humans were having such a good time, and Ariel was so interested in watching them, that no one noticed the black clouds racing toward the ship. In an instant, a great storm struck.

Roaring winds churned the ocean waves into mountains of water. Lightning bolts crackled across the darkened sky.

Ariel saw the crew lower a lifeboat and scramble into it. She saw Eric drop his dog Max overboard to safety. Then a huge explosion threw Eric into the raging sea.

Ariel let go of the storm-tossed ship and dove back into the sea. She darted through the waves to the side of the ship where Eric had fallen. He was gone! She plunged beneath the water and saw his sinking form. In an instant, she carried him to the surface and swam for shore.

The sudden storm had passed when Scuttle saw Ariel tugging the lifeless Eric onto the sandy beach.

"No pulse," Scuttle announced solemnly. "Dead as a Friggerzoid!" But Scuttle was wrong again.

"No, look! He's breathing," said Ariel. "Oh, he's so beautiful!" At that moment, Ariel knew she loved Eric. She began to sing. All at once, she saw his eyelids flutter.

Suddenly, Ariel heard Max bark, and knew that Prince Eric's friends would soon find him.

When Eric opened his eyes, Ariel was gone. All the young prince could remember was that someone had been with him. And she had been singing, in the most beautiful voice he had ever heard.

When Ariel got back to her cave, Eric was waiting for her. Not the real Eric. It was the statue of Eric she had seen on the ship. Flounder had rescued it for her.

"Oh, thank you, Flounder!" Ariel cried. "Oh, I do so love him!"

"Just wait until your father finds out about that!" Sebastian moaned.

Sebastian hadn't really meant to tell King Triton about Eric. It just sort of slipped out.

If Triton's anger had been an earthquake, it would have knocked the needle off the chart.

"You disobeyed me!" he said to Ariel. "I have no choice but to punish you."

He raised his magic trident. With a single terrifying blast, Triton destroyed all of Ariel's beloved human treasures. Even the statue of Eric.

From her palace, Ursula the Sea Witch had seen the destruction of Ariel's cave treasures. "I think the time is ripe," she said to her two slippery hench-eels, Flotsam and Jetsam.

Sobbing brokenly among her ruined treasures, Ariel suddenly discovered she had company.

"We know someone who can help you," hissed Flotsam.

"Who?" asked Ariel.

"Let's just say a friend," Jetsam hissed. "Come along and meet her."

"The solution to your problem is quite simple, my dear,"
Ursula said. "You love a human...so become a human
yourself."

"But how?" Ariel asked, her mermaid heart beating faster.

"No problem, Angelfish, as soon as you sign this contract."

"It says that I agree to make you a human for three days," Ursula explained. "If, after three days, Prince Eric does not love you, has not kissed you…you belong to me!

"Oh, yes—one other small matter. In exchange for my services, you are to give me…your voice."

"No, Ariel! Don't sign!" warned Sebastian. "Don't listen to her!"

"I must sign, Sebastian," Ariel said. "I love Eric. This is the only way."

"Smart girl," Ursula said, as Ariel signed the contract. "Now, let's get to work."

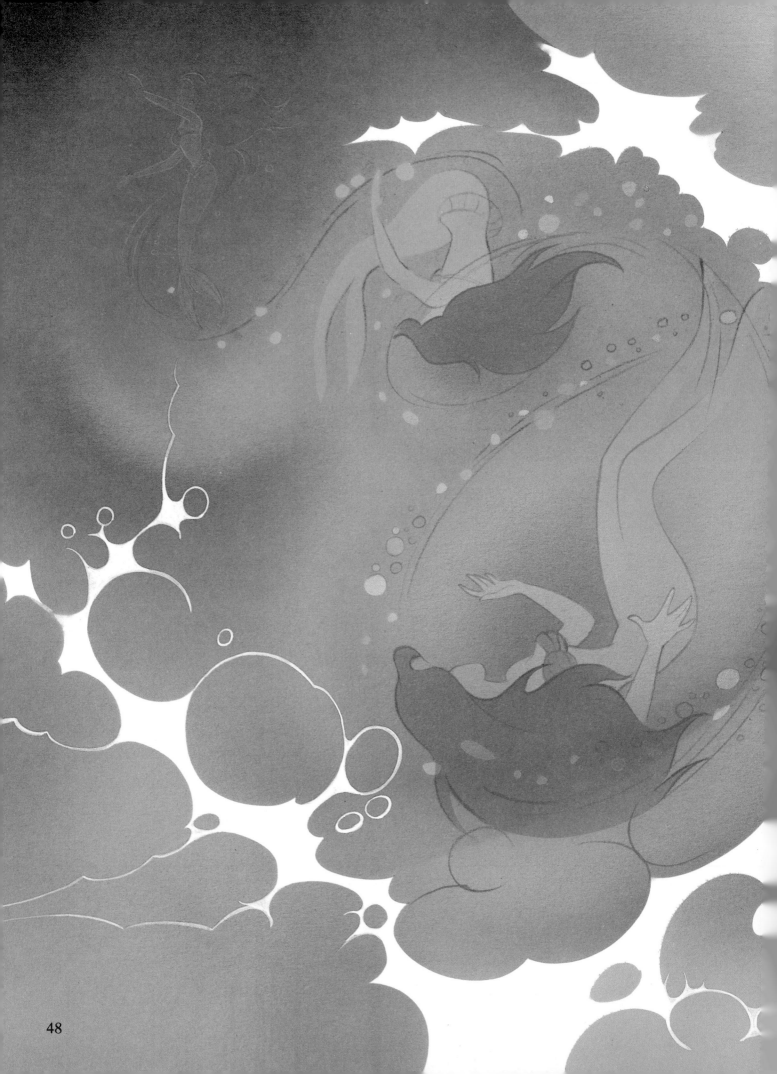

In the glow of Ursula's magic, the mermaid girl was slowly transformed. Then she began to gasp.

"Quick!" cried Sebastian to Flounder. "We must get her to the surface so she can breathe. She's not a mermaid anymore."

The next thing Ariel knew, she was on the beach.

"Hey!" Scuttle exclaimed. "What's goin' on, Ariel? Now, don't tell me…there's something different about you…" said the expert on humans.

"Ariel's not a mermaid anymore," Sebastian said. "She's got legs."

Since the day of the storm, Prince Eric had thought often of the mysterious golden voice he had heard. Who was the girl? Would he ever find her?

When he saw Ariel on the beach, his heart skipped a beat.

"Do I know you?" Eric said hopefully. Alas, Ariel could not answer.

"She cannot speak," Eric thought. "I guess she can't be the one."

But whoever she was, he could see that she was going to need help.

Eric took Ariel to his castle, where his servants fed her and gave her pretty clothes. Soon, everyone was wondering about Ariel. Who was this voiceless girl who combed her hair with a fork?

It was nearing the end of the first day. Sebastian had followed Ariel to the castle to help her if he could.

"You've only got two more days to get Eric to fall in love with you," the crab reminded her.

But Ariel wasn't paying attention. She was dreaming of her prince.

The next day, Eric ordered his coach and horses. "Let me show you my kingdom," he said to Ariel.

Ariel thought it was a beautiful kingdom, but she couldn't tell Eric.

The prince, on the other hand, was thinking, "What a beautiful girl! If only it had been her voice I heard!"

Three days had turned to two. Now, two days were turning to one. But now, everything was going to be all right. The flame of true love had been kindled in Eric's heart.

Later that day Eric took Ariel on a boat ride.

Suddenly, the boat in which Eric and Ariel were floating was overturned by Flotsam and Jetsam.

The romantic mood was shattered. Ariel didn't get her kiss, but she did get a dunking.

"That was a close call," Ursula said, watching the scene in her magic crystal ball. "It's time to take some drastic action."

In the twinkling of an eye, Ursula transformed herself into a beautiful young girl.

"With Ariel's voice and my looks, Triton's daughter and the prince will soon be mine," she gloated.

"Eric! I have come back to you," the transformed Ursula purred.

"That voice!" Eric cried. "It's you—my one true love!"

Using Ariel's stolen voice, Ursula had put Eric into a trance. Grimsby, his Chancellor, gasped in disbelief when Eric announced that he would marry this girl, who called herself Vanessa, that very night.

They would be married at sea, aboard Eric's ship. Alone in her cabin, the false Vanessa spoke to the real Ursula, reflected in the cabin mirror.

"Soon I'll have that little mermaid and her handsome prince, and the ocean will be mine."

Scuttle was peeking through the porthole, and he saw the Sea Witch's reflection. "I've gotta tell Ariel," he gasped.

On the shore, a brokenhearted Ariel looked out at the brightly decorated wedding ship—and at the setting sun of her final day as a human girl.

All at once, above her, she heard the excited voice of Scuttle. "Ariel! Vanessa is the Sea Witch—with your voice!"

"We've got to stop that wedding!" Sebastian exclaimed, leaping into action. "Flounder, get Ariel to the ship. I'll take care of the rest."

Scuttle, the first to arrive, led the attack on the wedding from sea and air.

The wedding guests scattered in confusion.

Sweeping down on Vanessa, Scuttle snatched from around her neck the shell necklace that contained Ariel's voice. When he dropped it on the deck of the ship, the shell broke. Freed from its shell prison, the voice returned to its rightful owner.

"Oh, Eric!" Ariel said.

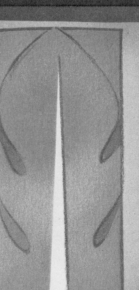
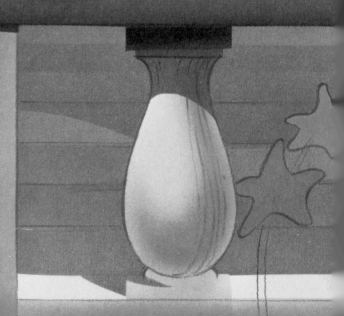

Eric took Ariel in his arms. "It was you all the time," he cried.

"Oh, Eric! I wanted to tell you…"

As the sun dipped below the horizon, Vanessa became the cackling Ursula again. "You're too late," she crowed. "You belong to me now!"

Ariel was a mermaid again.

"The sun has set on the third day!" Ursula shrieked triumphantly.

In a moment, both Ariel and Ursula had disappeared beneath the waves.

Eric leaped from the deck to a small boat tied below. In his hands, he held a sharp harpoon.

"I lost her once," he shouted to Grimsby. "I'm not going to lose her again!"

Alerted by Sebastian, Triton went to Ursula's grotto to bargain for his daughter's freedom.

"Very well, Triton," the Sea Witch said. "I'll give Ariel her freedom...in exchange for yours."

Triton had no choice. He yielded.

"At last!" Ursula crowed. "I am sole ruler of all the ocean!"

"You monster!" Ariel cried, clawing wildly at the Sea Witch. Ursula sidestepped the attack.

"Monster, eh? I'll show you a monster," she snarled.

And in a flash, with his own magic trident, Ursula transformed King Triton into a slimy, helpless sea creature and made him fast to the floor of her grotto.

Suddenly, Eric appeared. With a mighty heave, he sent his
harpoon flashing toward Ursula, wounding her.

Enraged, the Sea Witch aimed the magic trident at the prince.
At the last moment, Ariel threw Ursula off balance, and the
trident's beam hit Ursula's evil eels.

"Oh, my poor poopsies!" Ursula lamented over Flotsam and Jetsam. Then the Sea Witch's tears turned to rage. The fury in her evil heart grew, and so did she, until at last she towered above the surface of the ocean.

"You pitiful fools!" she shrieked. "Now you will feel the power of the Sea Witch!"

Lightning flashed. Great waves swept over the sea. In the tumult of Ursula's rage, shipwrecks on the bottom of the ocean were cast to the surface again.

Eric swam against the giant waves until, at last, he reached one of the dredged-up ships.

Somehow, Eric turned the ship and aimed the harpoonlike bowsprit at the heart of the mountainous sea witch. With a dreadful scream, she disintegrated into a patch of bubbling black ooze.

Ursula was gone, and with her, all the evil she had done. Triton was king of the seas again. And he granted Ariel her dearest wish—he made her human forevermore.

Triton watched Eric and Ariel walk toward Eric's castle. "You know, Sebastian," he finally said, "I'm going to miss her."

Eric and Ariel were married aboard
the wedding ship, with all the
merpeople looking on.

"I think they're going to live happily
ever after," said Scuttle.

And for once, Scuttle was right!

Published by
Penguin Books USA Inc.
375 Hudson Street
New York, New York, 10014

Produced by
Twin Books
15 Sherwood Place
Greenwich, CT 06830

ISBN 0-453-03075-0

Printed in Hong Kong

10 9 8 7 6 5 4 3 2 1